Ella Dietz, Koehler Collection of British Poetry

The Triumph of Love

a mystical poem in song, sonnets, and verse

Ella Dietz, Koehler Collection of British Poetry

The Triumph of Love
a mystical poem in song, sonnets, and verse

ISBN/EAN: 9783337382773

Printed in Europe, USA, Canada, Australia, Japan

Cover: Foto ©Andreas Hilbeck / pixelio.de

More available books at **www.hansebooks.com**

THE
TRIUMPH OF LOVE.

A
𝕸𝖞𝖘𝖙𝖎𝖈𝖆𝖑 𝕻𝖔𝖊𝖒
IN SONGS, SONNETS, AND VERSE.

BY
ELLA DIETZ.

LONDON:
E. W. ALLEN, 11, AVE MARIA LANE,
AND STATIONERS' HALL COURT.
MDCCCLXXVII.

LOAN STACK

𝕴 believed, and therefore have 𝕴 spoken.

▲ 2

Prologue.

Two hearts whose love no words can e'er express,
Laid down their outward life that they might be
United in one heart of holiness.
Shall not that heart, O world, gain love from thee?
May it not win all souls to tenderness,
And fill all human hearts with charity,
That they may see in love's deep sacredness
The very source and soul of purity?
If I unveil the workings of that heart,
It is, O brothers, that your eyes may see
How sin doth bring us every woe and smart,
Until 'tis conquered by love's unity;
And fight once fought, the crown's for ever won,
For what God doeth cannot be undone!

L'Envoi.

PLIGHT me no troth, pledge me no word;
Should I clip the wings of my forest bird?
　　　Soar high, fly free,
　　　Thy soul is with me.

　　　All thy heart feels
　　　Of pleasure or pain,
　　　O'er my heart steals
　　　Like an echoed refrain;
　　　When thine eyes shall afar
　　　Seek the beam of some star
　　　In the soft southern night,
　　　I shall feel too its light.

Tuning the Harp.

My heart so wrought upon by grief and woe,
Had longed for death, and sought to meet his face,
The peaceful goal of life's long weary race,—
When suddenly great joy did overthrow
My grief; and o'er me bliss did flow
In roseate rapturous flames; my pain gave place
To such intense delight,—for Heaven's sweet grace
I cried—more happiness I dared not know.

For all my veins seemed filled with liquid fire,
And every nerve, like harp-strings stretched and
     strung,
Vibrated harmonies that angels sung.
My flesh seemed cloven asunder by desire
To melt my soul for evermore in thine,
And be with thee absorbed in the Divine.

The Key Note.

Look on me with thy calm unpitying eyes,
Thy strength doth make me strong ; thou would'st
    not move,
Though I should lie here slain of thee and love ;
Thou art not tender, but thou art most wise,
And thou canst bear the flame that purifies,
And brave the fire divine, and dare to prove
The power of pinions made to soar above,
And bring down hidden blessings from the skies.
For Love has ruled the earth, and ruled the sea,
And shall not Love control the heavenly air,
Whose throne is builded in the starry heights ?
There are no barriers to spirits free,
No ways but highways to two souls that dare;
Nor time, nor space, nor death, nor days, nor nights.

Part I.

RETROSPECTION.

Sweet wiǹed Hypnos closed my eyes,
And soothed my weary brain,
And there reflected mirror-wise
The old new life again.

I DREAMED that thou and I, near the white Throne,
Heard from afar the wail of earth's deep moan,
And kneeling down before the Hidden Face
We prayed for power, for sustenance, for grace—
That we might go as messengers of love,
Bearing the healing branch the Mystic Dove,
The Comforter, had plucked from life's fair tree,
The branch of peace.   The power to us was given ;
And thou swift dropt to earth, I dwelt in heaven,
Watching afar to guide the soul of thee.

O take my hand, and let me dream again
Of that abode of bliss above earth's pain.

Ah, but 'twas bitter grief to watch thee so.
Amid the joys of heaven I felt thy woe ;

Among the angel choir I could not sing,
I could not tune my harp's discordant string
Vibrating to thy heart's deep piteous sighs;
And through the rainbow clouds I saw thine eyes
Tear-stained and grieving.   O that face of thine!
That beauteous face, that erst was wont to shine
With heaven's own light; so pure the Holy One
Might loving gaze and claim thee for His son;
So sorrow-changed I scarce should know thee now,
Save for the circling flame upon thy brow
That e'en the fires of hell could not destroy;
Thy voice, once loud amid the choir of praise,
But sobbed an echo of earth's nights and days,
And I stood lone in heaven without one joy.

> *Clasp close my hand, and tearful eyes keep dry;*
> *We shall return to bliss beyond the sky.*

At length, so weary grew I of the place,
I knelt again before the Hidden Face,
Praying that I might go and be with thee;
And by the prayer I felt my soul set free,
And slowly sinking with my weight of tears
Toward dark earth, down through the crystal spheres,
Winding in spiral whirls, to some low spot
I came; I came, but oh! I found thee not;
Lost was my harp, lost was my heavenly crown;
I cried aloud, " Where art thou, oh my own ? "

No voice made answer, and I stood alone ;
Stifled by airy seas, but could not drown.

Hold me within thine arms, that I may see
The end of death, despair, and misery.

I found myself a strange and lonely child,
And heard far voices sigh in forests wild—
Saw shadowy forms gleam in the misty air ;
Sweet chords of harmony and visions rare
Haunted my days and nights ; I could not sleep ;
I heard the deep low calling unto deep,
I gazed above and saw the starry lyre,
The constellations set, the crown of fire,
The deep blue of night's sky, the blue of seas,
The radiance of the moon, and heard the breeze
Sobbing through tall straight pines ; my being
   yearned
To clasp this beauteous life ; my pulses burned
To sing again some sweet forgotten strain ;
To hear some voice echo my heart's refrain ;
This longing was the pain within my bliss,
This was the thorn that grew 'neath every rose,
This was the aching cord I could not miss,
The dream that ever held me from repose.

Close, close, O clasp me close ; found, found at last,
The memory of earth's grief is fading fast !

I grew from childhood, stood confronting fate,
Deep eyes sought mine, I heard of love and hate,
Saw war and bloodshed, death, despair, and crime,
Race against race, and sacrifice sublime
For liberty, and heard the loud applause
Wrung from a nation's heart in freedom's cause ;
Saw thousands march to death, saw the return
Of veteran ranks blood-stained, felt my heart burn
At sight of their grim faces row on row,
And all the ghastly truth I seemed to know
Of brothers lying dead on battle fields ;
I heard deep groans, the groans the body yields
While giving up the soul ; and ache for ache
I felt their pain, and died for freedom's sake
With them again, and gladly would die so
In verity, to ease earth of its woe.

Lay thy hand here upon my aching heart,
For soul and body are so fain to part.

I travelled northward o'er the inland seas,
To where the red Aurora swept and burned,
And Indian faces which the white man spurned
Beneath his feet, I saw ; and mighty trees,
And rivers, and the wide stretched prairie land,
Waving with flowers, a purple sea when fanned
By rippling winds, a golden, when the sun
Shed slanting beams before the day was done.

And gay young faces gathered round me there,
And brave young hearts loved mine, and loved me
    well ;
I could not rest though all the land was fair,
No hand had power my heart's dream to dispel.

    The wide earth holds for me no place of rest,
    Save this within thy heart, upon thy breast.

There came a time of trial, words of fire
Should paint the dread volcano's lava streams ;
Another will crossed mine with stern desire,
An actual life combatted with my dreams.
Child ! still a child facing the problem human,
And burdened with the anguish of the woman.

    Sweet love, give o'er, for death is over-sweet :
    No more, no more, lest love die at death's feet.

Some years of patient bearing of the load,
Turning my nature to another's will,
Speaking soft words, smiling beneath the goad,
Wondering to see my good revert to ill,
Hiding my sorrow with a conscious pride,
Striving with gentleness to help, to guide :
The flower of duty grew where love would not ;
I watered with my tears the lovely spot.

And thou wert in the world and gave no sign,
But through the darkness my soul called to thine.

Across the sea, a waif tossed by the spray
Of chance, I sailed, saw the land fade away—
My native land—and smiled, nor shed one tear.
Did my heart whisper I was drawing near
To thee ?   I know not, but to me the seas
Sang only songs of joy, deep harmonies
Of peace, the sea-gulls gleamed against the sky ;
Afar, anear, down-dropping, drawing nigh,
Their white plumes seemed like omens of good cheer ;
My free soul loved the sea and laughed at fear.
O the bright glory of those starry nights !
The surging gulfs, the phosphorescent fires,
The foam illumined by soft glowing lights
Within the waves, the tall mast's slender spires,
The sailor's rhythmèd songs, the wind-filled sails,
The strong ship's speeding spite of threatening gales.
Stars, skies, seas, songs, winds, waves, were dear to
    me !
O ecstasy of life !   O liberty !

As tempest draws the sky to sea's embrace,
So fate drew me hungering to greet thy face.

Some months amid the ruins of the past,
Some weeks like years, some hours like crowded days,

Some moments pregnant with eternities,
Some blisses sweet, too brief, too sweet to last ;
My heart stood still, dumb with unuttered praise,
Beholding childhood's dreams realities.
From my own land where the great golden sun
Shed gorgeous hues upon the sunset clouds—
Those airy temples built by mists and winds—
I came, unknowing all that man had done
To liberate the soul that nature shrouds,
To grasp the jewel which all nature binds ;
All the wild worship that my soul had known,
I saw reflected in man's prayers of stone.

Doth not the heavenly choir above us bend,
While our two souls aspire, adore, ascend ?

Dear England, how I love thy fields and lakes !
However fair thy gracious daughter be,
My heart in gratitude must turn to thee,
Sweet Mother ! for thy deep heart throbs and aches
In unison with all humanity ;
Thou art the fount from which we drew our life,
Thy red blood in our veins doth seethe and burn,
The liberty that grew from out our strife
But proves us doubly thine ; for thee we yearn,
We yield allegiance to thy loving heart
That thou couldst never conquer by thy sword ;

Let seas roll mountains high, we cannot part,
For we are one in thought, and deed, and word.

As thou and I, dear heart, as thou and I
May now clasp hands through earth, and sea, and
sky.

Interlude.

Pausing.

HENCEFORTH, O love, I shut the world's wide door,
That thou and I may in the garden dwell
Alone, alone, no heaven for us, nor hell,
But rest eternal by the golden shore.
We hear afar the cherubim adore,
Our answering hearts repeat the rhythmed swell ;
But harps lie idle, nor can dumb lips tell
The joys of silence, ours for evermore.
Immortal youth is ours, we smile at Fate,
All seasons melt to everlasting Spring,
And God-like power is ours to will and wait :
Time is our servant, it shall surely bring
All treasures to our feet to consecrate
Unto our Lord, our ever-living King.

Part II.

INTROSPECTION.

Sursum Corda.

I LOVE thee, but mine eyes are set
Away from thee, above, beyond,
For O, my own, I am too fond,
And seeing thee I might forget
To worship at the holier shrine,
And praise the Power that made thee mine.

It is so sweet, so sweet to see
The tender light within thine eyes,
The swift bright gleam of glad surprise,
And joy that sometimes greeteth me :
Yet that deep radiance, I know,
Doth from a greater glory flow.

It is so sweet to feel thy heart
Surround me with its loving ways ;
But when I think what lonely days,
O love, have held our souls apart,
I long to end this weary race,
And sink with thee in death's embrace.

No ! our two souls must upward rise,
And worship at the starry throne ;
Our double hearts must beat as one,
Our prayers conjoined must pierce the skies ;
Till we reflect God's glory here,
We cannot pass to His bright sphere.

I.

WHEN first I saw thee my poor eyes were blind,
And only saw thy face, and could not see
Thy inner soul—the hidden part of me—
My other self, which now at last I find ;
And having found again, I clasp and bind,
And hold thee close, and merge myself in thee ;
Our souls are one above eternally,
And shall be one on earth, in heart and mind.
For me all truth lies hid within thine eyes,
Deep wells of light from whence life's currents flow.
Look on me, love, if thou would'st have me wise,
Light me with love, if thou would'st have me know
The heights and depths of heavenly mysteries,
For thou on me all knowledge canst bestow.

II.

I am thy dove,—ay, call me by that name;
My soul is pure and free within thy sight,

And spreads its snowy pinions to the light,
Nor fears to bask within the rosy flame.
Thy wild wood dove that heard thy voice, and came
Swift through the darkness and the silent night,
Bringing new comfort in its circling flight,
Seeking its own, its lost mate to reclaim.
What though the journey were so dark with woe,
And my poor plumes in grievous struggles torn,
If at the last I meet and overthrow
The adverse fate ?   If my strong courage, born
Of many griefs, bring us to see and know
The heavenly way, we'll laugh the past to scorn !

III.

Should we part now ?   O love, how can we part?
Leave if thou wilt, thou canst not take away
The glory and the brightness of the day;
My soul will be with thine where'er thou art :
Till thou canst send the red blood from thy heart
Thou canst not banish me, though I may stay
As silently ; still shall my silence pray
Until thy spirit feel the vital smart.
I would not have thee suffer, O my own,
I would not hold thee, thou shouldst still be free,
For when thou goest I am not alone,
Thou canst not take thyself away from me :
But thou canst dim the brightness of the sun
With clouds.   O love ! I would not have thee gone !

Crowned.

Your kisses fell upon my face,
As soft and light as flakes of snow
Fall on the frozen earth below,
And rest there for a little space,
Before the summer roses blow.

My spirit stood as if apart,
Watching the body of one dead,
But yet I heard each word you said,
And felt the throbbing of your heart,
Though from my heart all life seemed fled.

Your dear lips went from chin to brow,
And left a circling ring of flame,
And at each touch a cherub came,
And breathed some sweet unspoken vow;
Methought each kiss a cherub's name.

And now I nevermore am lone,
Upon my forehead gleams the light
Of one transcendent jewel bright,
And angels sing around the Throne
Of that blest coronation night.

Interlude.

MINOR CHORDS.

Doubting.

Is it a dream, O love! only a dream
That we have met and loved ?   Am I awake ?
I who once thought thy heart's great thirst to slake?
I who once sought the lost past to redeem,
Now see dark shadows where was wont to gleam
The morning's light all golden for thy sake—
For thou, my blest one, thou hadst power to make
The grayest dawn brighter than sun's bright beam.
Our love-song seemed so full of harmony,
Breathing of tuneful birds, and happy spring,
I never thought what discord there might be
Beneath for thee,—nay, thou shalt never sing
In pity, nor for grace ; go ! thou art free !
Would God I ne'er had stayed thy flying wing !

Hope Lost.

I'LL now no more believe that summer sun
Doth shine, that skies are blue, that roses blow—
I'll only say, " It seemeth to be so,"
At dawn I'll think, " Perchance the day's begun,"
But if black night with swifter pace doth run
And overtake,—it may be so I know,—
I'll wonder not ; since joy might turn to woe
In briefer space, and hearts be twain being one.
Vague memories, links to a golden past
Thou hast recalled, forgotten days of yore
In other lives, before dark Fate had cast
Our souls beyond the gates,—O that blest shore !
I dreamed its golden strand was won at last—
Nay, sleep, belovëd ! I shall dream no more.

The Passion.

My body suffers even unto death,
My heavy cross, too heavy seems to bear ;
Alas, alas ! I have no strength to wear
My crown of thorns, I draw reluctant breath,
And every nerve and fibre murmureth
Against my life ; O Lord, how shall I dare
To drink thy cup ?   Spare me, I cry—O spare
This bitter hour.   The silence answereth.
Father, not my will, but thy will be done ;
Thine is the kingdom, glory, and the power ;
Thine is the victory, if race be won ;
Thine is the triumph, in this darkest hour ;
My God ! my God ! hast thou forsaken me ?
O Christ, I drink thy cup of agony !

Chorus.

O VIRGIN soul, sit free,
He shall return to thee—
Thy dove, thy spouse :
Sit at the heavenly gate,
Possess thy soul, and wait
What God allows !

The Thread Resumed.

Faith Restored.

It may be, love, that I alone must sing,
It may be, love, that I alone must see
The promised good—the possibility
That broods above us with its sheltering wing :
But if thy heart, at last awakening,
Send back its wealth of answering strength to me,
O what a double power our lives will be ;
How will harmonious chords vibrate and ring.
Until that time I'll never cease to pray
That we two, guided by the Shepherd's voice,
May walk together in the narrow way
That leadeth unto life ; may we rejoice
In pastures green, and by still waters stray,
Until our Father's will become our choice.

The Sacrament.

The Lord hath shown to me this mystery :—
Control the flesh if we would free the spirit,
Subdue this world and we shall then inherit
All things, and clothed with immortality

Shall cry, "O grave ! where is thy victory ?
O death ! where is thy sting ?" Then shall we merit
The crown of glory here, and then shall wear it,
Tuning our harps beside the molten sea.
The man and woman joined but in the Lord
Shall feel the all-pervading essence roll
In them, and through them ; the Incarnate Word
Revealed in flesh, all flesh shall then control.
As thou for me the sacred wine hast poured,
I break my body up to feed thy soul.

Creation.

Thou wert created first, and I from thee :
As 'twas of old in the primeval man,
So now by the new type doth nature plan
To work her will through us unconsciously.
What thou hast lost thou find'st again in me,
And in my being thou thyself may'st scan.
I was within thee ere thy life began,
And what thou art, look in my face and see
Soul of thy soul I am, heart of thy heart :
Let not the fire upon the altar perish :
High Priest art thou, and I thy counterpart,
The Temple of the Lord ; and thou should'st cherish
And keep the holy place, where the bright flame
Consumes the sacrifice—reveals His Name.

Love's Worship.

Thy lips to me have never said " I love."
Perchance thy heart hath never breathed a vow
Unto itself, yet I behold thee now
So near to me—my white one !   O my dove !
How thy strong pinions seem to bend above !
Thy murmured blessings kiss my cheek and brow—
Thou art above me sometimes, O allow
Me too to worship, and thy godhead prove.
Nay, do not feel thine own unworthiness,
But search thyself to see what I divine,
And bring the treasure forth to save and bless ;
If I discover it, the pearl is mine ;
And for my worship do not hold me less :
'Tis my divinity that shows me thine.

Love's Strength.

I sometimes feel that I am strong to bear
All things, belovèd one, for thy dear sake.
Even to stand aside and see thee take
Blessings from other hands—to see thee wear
A crown not of my weaving : if thou dare
To enter hell, my faith it will not shake.

Brave all temptations, they I know but make
More resolute thy will, thy soul more fair.
When thou hast searched the universe all through,
And failed alone to find the central thought,
Watch where the needle points,—'twill lead thee
    true :
Gain thou this knowledge howe'er dearly bought,
That thou the whole art powerless to construe,
Until by thine own centre thou art taught.

Love's Sympathy.

My lonely one, thou never more art lone,
My living spirit vibrates through thy frame,
Mine eyes have pierced the veil : I overcame
By love, and by its art my thoughts have flown
And read thy wishes : thy soul's wants are known
To me before thou givest them a name ;
My actual presence scarce could yield the same
Unbroken sympathy ; till hearts have grown
To throb as one, silence is sometimes best,
For speech the inmost soul cannot reveal,
And when thought answers thought, true lovers rest
In that deep peace, forgetting woe or weal :
'Tis like a child upon its mother's breast—
Blest unity where God hath set His seal.

Love's Prescience.

I CLOSED my outer eyes that I might see
Thy inner self revealed to inner sight,
And from mine eyes went forth electric light
That seemed to penetrate the soul of thee,
And radiate from thence ; thou wert to me
A shell wherein I dwelt, a clothing bright,
That warmed and covered me ; I felt I might
Do aught, and yet I felt that both were free.
We were together but was neither lost,
Each seemed to hold a separate essence still ;
I throbbed through thee, and thou didst me enfold,
And all was harmony, no wish was crossed,
No strife, nor yielding to another's will.
This sight I now shall evermore behold !

Love's Power.

I HOLD thee in the hollow of my hand;
I draw thee as the magnet draws the pole
Opposed to it; and thus, love, soul to soul
We two together evermore shall stand.
For what can sunder us?   Nor sea nor land,
Since we can pierce the universal whole
Like subtle ether ; we unseen control
Our destinies ; and work what God hath planned.
If on the earth our feet can find no place,
Then we perforce must seek the upper air :
I'll brave all heights, so we stand face to face,
All clouds, all dangers, if thou art but there ;
I think God sent us from His Throne of grace
The power of love to prove and to declare.

Interlude.

THE VALLEY OF THE SHADOW.

Sunset.

I WONDER if thine eyes will ever rest
Upon these words that my poor hand hath writ
Watching afar ; still lonely I must sit,
While thoughts fly to thee, as birds fly to nest
At eventide ; thou art my dream, my quest,
The answer to myself, my opposite,
My golden sun before whose beams shades flit,
The motor of my life, its goal, its zest.
I fain would clasp thee, love, before I go
Across the river—if perchance it be
That I must cross—these heights of Alpine snow
Have made me worthier heaven and worthier thee,
And if I die, 'tis not in vain, I know,
I die believing love's great mystery.

The Afterglow.

My loved one, when thou'rt near I feel too much,
Mine eyes are dazzled by thy golden beams;
I dare not look upon my wondrous dream's
Fulfilment; and my heart-strings 'neath thy touch
Do quiver so—my music, 'tis but such
As th' Eolian harp doth make, and thus it seems
Half discord, broken harmonies, and streams
Of melodies we strive in vain to clutch.
But when thou goest, 'tis as when the sun
Leaves all his splendor in the western skies,
And one may gaze and gaze and fill one's eyes
With glory: the real day is never done
But melts into the night: O glad surprise!
The myriad stars repeat the song begun!

My Knight.

O THOU dost love me with a perfect strength—
With strength to crown and bless, and still forbear
To gather aught, and thus my heart at length
Hath found a voice and courage to declare,
Because that thou canst give and yet withhold—
Because thy will can conquer and subdue
The elemental force that doth enfold
My spirit ; now it leaps to life anew
Beneath thy touch ! yea, sleeping, I have lain ;
A fell enchantment struggled for my life,
But thou art come and the enchanter slain—
Bleeding and vanquished 'neath thy piercing knife.
So enter thou the castle of my heart :
Lord of its treasure, my true knight thou art.

Recalled.

I thought thy rival death would take me first,
He almost stole my body quite away,
And I resisted not; I longed to burst
All earthly bonds and dwell above this clay ;
And I thought smiling, "Though death hold me
    fast,
My soul can freely go to him I love ;
Then shall all struggling cease, all grief be past,
When I can watch him evermore above."
But thou hast called my spirit back again,
And bid'st me from the bonds of death go free.
Yea, I will bear this body and its pain,
If soul and body both are dear to thee ;
And through this earthly form my soul shall shine :
Since thou dost love me, I am *all* divine.

Part III.

THE REALITY.

D

I.

It matters not, if thou wert false to me,
The heavenly legions would protect my soul;
And I can rest in God, if not in thee;
Thou art a part of His eternal whole;
And 'twas His likeness in thee that I saw:
But if thou trample out the face divine,
Thou art the loser, God's unchanging law
Remains, His glory will for ever shine;
His hand alone has power to take or give;
We illustrate His will in all we do:
Though thou should'st slay me, He can make me
    live,—
Yea, make me live, and slay the slayer too:
He offers thee His mercy, but be sure,
Though thou reject it, justice will endure.

II.

Nay, do not pity me that I do love:
Pity thyself, and thy poor piteous fear,
That cramps and holds, nor lets thee soar above
This dull and darksome earth and its low sphere.

Look at yon bird cleaving the radiant air ;
What is the tempest or the night to him ?
And dost thou pity him ? or dare compare
Thine eyes with his no blazing sun can dim ?
Oh, I thank God that I have heart to feel
And power to suffer,—if He wills it so,—
And courage all my suffering to reveal—
The concentrated cry of woman's woe.
Lay down thy heart, thy soul, thy life for me ;
Till then thy pity and thyself go free.

III.

Thou know'st that 'tis no passion of the blood,
That thus hath drawn me, love, unto thy feet,—
Nay, 'tis the very strength of womanhood ;
The love of love that doth all life complete.
My soul can speak to thine from furthest space,
As light greets light, and star doth answer star ; .
And 'tis my soul that leads me to thy face,
Because thine eyes cannot yet see afar.
Why wilt thou wander in the darkness still ?
Why dost thou fear and shun the heavenly light ?
O, love, my love, renounce thy wayward will !
Must I too follow through the doleful night ?
Canst thou not see the shining god of day ?
Then thou art blind, and shalt not lead the way !

" I know a song which I need only to sing when men have loaded me with bonds : when I sing it, my chains fall in pieces, and I walk forth at liberty."

Song.

Those starry eyes! those starry eyes!
  Light me through night with light of love ;
And when on earth their radiance dies,
  Methinks they'll light the heavens above.

Their piercing rays! their piercing rays!
  Have called my spirit from afar ;
Can I forget those deathless days
  When we two dwelt in one bright star ?

I float away ! I float away !
  I feel no care, I have no will ;
Thine eyes alone can bid me stay,
  Mine answering soul obeys them still.

O eyes to eyes! and soul to soul!
  When shall we twain again be one?
Revolving as a perfect whole
  Around the burning central sun.

Oh, lost estate ! Oh, lost estate!
  Shall we regain our matehood here,
And banish death, and conquer fate,
  And form anew our starry sphere ?

Love's Wealth.

O, I AM rich beyond all power to tell,
For I can open now highways and gates,
Nought can resist the all-compelling spell,
The concentrated strength of blended fates ;
And I have endless stores of wealth within,
Waiting the magic touch of thy dear hand ;
When glorious sun appears the buds begin
To open, and the blossoms to expand.
Since thou hast crowned me, I am queen indeed ;
My royal will leaps over bonds and bars ;
I can command the elements at need,
And claim allegiance from the very stars,
And all mankind shall see what thou hast done, —
Crowned me with light, and clothed me with the
    sun !

Charity.

I FEEL that I would draw all souls on earth
To th' universal love, the Mother's breast,
The fount of life that gives us all new birth,
The bosom on which all alike may rest ;
The Comforter, the reconciling Dove,
That broods for ever o'er the soul of man,
And draws us upward spirally : above
Mysteriously working inner plan.

That is the love that seems beyond all law,
The solvent that transmutes all things to good ;
Jerusalem the free, that prophets saw:
The Mother-God, that none have understood ;
The mystery of godliness revealed,
Which from the earliest ages hath been sealed.

Song.

Good night, good night, parting is such sweet sorrow,
That I shall say good night till it be morrow.

Romeo and Juliet. Shakspeare. Act II. Scene II.

THOU say'st " Good night !"   My heart replies
.Good night, good night ! and once again,
Good night to lips, good night to eyes ;
God keep thee, love, from all love's pain ;
God keep thee, love, since we must part:
      Good night, sweet heart !

And still I say to lips and eyes,
" Good night, good night !"—'tis sweetest pain ;
My very soul within me dies,
I strive to let thee go in vain ;
God help us, love, if we must part:
      Good night, sweet heart ! .

And God will help, my weakness flies,
I feel all strength to bear love's pain;
I pray that He will keep those eyes,
And bring them back to me again;
So joined in Him we cannot part:
      Good night, sweet heart!

I.

I STAND and wait beside the heavenly gate
Alone, alone, I cannot enter in,
For till thy soul meet mine I needs must wait;
We must together stand, pure, free from sin,
Naked and unashamed; the flaming sword
Hath kept us long from our lost Paradise;
Yet Thou wast crucified for us, O Lord!
Thou hast redeemed and bought us with a price;
Thou hast declared that we are not our own,
And hast commanded us to image Thee,
And yet we will not kneel before the throne;
We still reject the truth that makes all free:
O Father, give me strength, till serpent's head
Lie crushed beneath my heel—bruised, bleeding,
    dead!

Song.

O TOUCH me not, unless thy soul
   Can claim my soul as thine ;
Give me no earthly flowers that fade,
   No love, but love divine :
For I gave thee immortal flowers,
That bloomed serene in heavenly bowers.

Look not with favour on my face,
   Nor answer my caress,
Unless my soul have first found grace
   Within thy sight ; express
Only the truth, though it should be
Cold as the ice on northern sea.

O never speak of love to me,
   Unless thy heart can feel
That in the face of Deity
   Thou wouldst that love reveal :
For God is love, and His bright law
Should find our hearts without one flaw.

Waiting.

PENELOPE sat weaving all the day
Her web ; and I weave mine of tender thought,
And many a quaint device by me is wrought
Of Fancy's golden threads.   What will he say
When he shall come ?   Will he entreat and pray
To see the legend ?   Will his heart be taught
By it ?   Night comes and brings me nought ;
I must unweave ; Ulysses is away.
But when my hero shall at last have come,
And his dear eyes have proved my colours true,
I wonder, will my stammering lips be dumb,
My heart's great love unspoken ?   Then must you,
Dear woven thing, help eyes and blushing cheek
To tell him all I feel, but cannot speak.

Day Song.

Wake ! wake ! the dawn is breaking,
  The doves are cooing low,
And love my heart is taking
  To where the lilies blow ;
My love is there awaking
  From blessed dreams, I know.

Wake ! wake ! the wind is sighing,
  With love from hill to plain.
Wake ! wake ! the night is dying,
  Glad day has come again.
O, hear my heart replying
  To thy dear heart's refrain.

Wake ! wake ! the night is over,
  The birds sing in the groves,
The bees hum o'er the clover,
  And every wild thing roves.
O wake, my dreaming lover,
  And hear how my heart loves !

Song.

Take thou the joy, O love, give me the sorrow,
For sweet love's pain is sweet, its sharpest sting
Hath such renewing strength, that I may borrow
From its red wounds the life wherewith I sing.

Dream brightest dreams, O love, e'en though the
    morrow
Should prove those dreams untrue, then let night
    bring
Sleep and oblivion, love, I'll wake with sorrow,
So peace but cover thee with sheltering wing.

If love's red fruit be always veined with sorrow,
Drain thou the sweetness, love, and backward fling
Wild tears and torturing pain; wake on the morrow
To hear my song's exultant answering.

"The kingdom of heaven is like unto a merchantman seeking goodly pearls, who, when he had found one pearl of great price, went and sold all that he had and bought it."

MATT. xiii. 45, 46.

Song.

I would die for my love, I would die for thee,
I would walk the earth barefoot through wind and
  rain ;
For love is my life, and my liberty,
I have gained its bliss, I can bear its pain.

I.

WE stand together, love, and hand in hand
We walk a path no other feet have trod ;
On either side is death, the summit grand,
Flames with the awful glory of our God :
And unseen foes beset us on the way—
The elemental force, and powers of air,
The prince of darkness—oh stand close and pray ;
Steep is the way and dark the winding stair.
We leave the valley far below, the world
Spreads out beneath us at our very feet,
Above, the thunderbolts of heaven are hurled,
The tempter's voice says " Worship me, complete
Your kingdom here."—" Get thee behind us, slave,
Our Lord and God alone has power to save."

II.

Upon my knees, my own, upon my knees
I read thy letter, and the sweet words seem
Less real than the visions of my dream.
As one who gazes o'er the barren seas
Till eyes grow dim, I watched; the welcome breeze
At last blows nearer one white sail, a gleam
Of light against the sky's deep blue, a beam
Of promise; then heart fails, and vision flees.
O what God shows us we are strong to bear;
The wondrous sight I saw and did not quail,
Our radiant souls woven of sun and air,
 Could interpenetrate the inner veil;
But now—I almost faint—O wilt thou dare?
Be strong, courageous heart, we must not fail !

Song.

Not for myself I claim thee,
But oh, for the suffering world,
Though the same world should blame thee,
Though its dark scorn be hurled
Alike on thy head and mine,
Forgive with a mercy divine !
Think of our Lord who died,
Think of Him, crucified !

I.

YIELD up to me, thy heart, thy soul, thy will,
As I have yielded up myself on high;
Our crystal sphere might then reflect the sky,
And here on earth the higher law fulfil,
Command the tempest with our " Peace, be still,"
Call down the heavenly power that draweth nigh,
Lay hold on God and make Him hear our cry,
Till with new life divine our beings thrill.
Oh that first sin! Shall it not be forgiven?
Must we for ever hear the tempter's voice?
And wilt thou suffer it till seventy times seven?
Oh Lord, redeem this flesh! make us rejoice
In serving thee, Thy law write on our heart,
Come dwell within us, Lord, no more depart!

II.

O WHAT is love? Love is the breath of heaven,
The light of light, and the consuming fire;
Love is the thunderbolt that Jove was given.
Love is a yearning anguish, a desire,
For love hath every form and every feature,
It shineth in the star and in the worm —
The life of life, the soul of every creature,
The impulse of the planet and the germ.

Love is transmutable, controls all forces,
Commands the elements, and they obey,
Can wrench the stars themselves from out their
    courses,
Is unsubduable, hath power to slay,
And whoso drinketh deep of love divine,
Shall see how through all law love's light doth shine.

III.

O WE must guard our love with jealous care ;
Remember, O my own, its heavenly birth,
Created by the sun and radiant air,
It cannot rest upon this struggling earth.
But we may fly with it to realms of light,
A thousand glorious joys await us there
Above the clouds, above the dolorous night,
'Mid starry flowers of heaven, and visions rare !
There soul to soul we float through endless space,
Upborne by etheric waves, we pass through stars ;
Upon thy heart I rest, in thy embrace,
And cradled thus no element debars ;
The universal force upon us waits --
And voices cry, " Open, ye heavenly gates."

Song.

Subdue the tempest of the blood
　　That is the earthly element,
Then shall the great electric flood
　　Through every nerve and fibre blent,
Reflect His image on each heart,
And make us all of Him a part.

I.

I feel so earnestly the truth I sing,
I cannot stop to think about the tune :
A thousand roses blow in fruitful June,
A thousand roses I must cull and fling
Before new Love where she comes conquering :
There is no time to trim, arrange, and prune ;
Before Love's feet all flowers are opportune,
Bring garlands wild, and song-birds sing on wing.
For Love is born again, O sorrowing world!
Rejoice! rejoice! with pæans to the skies;
To the white flag of peace at last unfurled!
Creation sounds the trump, and heaven replies.
Lo the lost orbit whence we have been hurled,
See the glad earth once more triumphant rise !

E.

Song.

I sat beneath the shadowy trees,
And watched their tops swayed by the breeze :
Two nests stood out against the sky,
Two pairs of happy birds on high ;—
Would we were birds, love, thou and I.

I wandered slowly through the rain,
My soul subdued by all earth's pain,
Its human life so full of woe :
How came we here ? when shall we go ?
I would that thou and I might know.

True Worship.

Dᴇᴀʀ is the light of thine eyes to me,
   Sacred the touch of thy lips;
And the sight of thy face as the sight of land
   To those on storm-tossed ships.
Should I not love thee, when I love the whole
Of thy strong, perfect loving soul?

Dear is the light of the stars to me,
   Sacred the light of the sun,
Their brightness shines as the shining Face
   Of the great Eternal One:
Should I not love these, when I love the whole
Of the Omnipresent Living Soul?

Song.

A THOUSAND birds in gilded cages sing,
   I sing alone beneath a wintry sky,
With only heart and voice for offering,
   But these I humbly yield to the Most High;
A simple strain sung in a simple way,
As if a child should lift its voice to pray.

But O, my brothers, though so great in singing,
   You have not the one truth I fain would sing;
See, 'tis a woman's heart that now is bringing
   Her choral wreaths before sweet Love to fling:
Sad was the song you sang in the old day,
My love triumphant comes to bless, not slay.

Song.

If sin could be sinless, our sin would be,
　Could we so fall, but the better way
　Our feet have found, and we cannot stray,
Though our souls are free as the air is free.
We've nought to forget, nought to forgive,
Nought to regret, only to live
　In the light of the endless day.

I.

How long my heart hath hungered, love, for thee !
How long I held thee in my spirit arms,
And sought to shield thy life by mystic charms !
I thought thy fate would take thee over sea,
And while I held thee so, I left thee free ;
Free from myself and from my weak alarms,
Free from all selfish love that blights and harms,
And thus true faith hath gained the victory.
True faith and stainless love, so purified
From earthly taint or shade of earthly dross,
I sometimes think my body must have died,
Since I can feel no more the body's cross :
God hath removed the curse from thee and me,
And writ the perfect law of liberty.

II.

I LIKE to hear thee read and praise my verse:
'Tis but the shadow cast by thine own light,
And could not live at all but in thy sight;
But O, I would not have the power reverse ;
'Tis well for me our love to intersperse
With songs and ditties and sweet sayings bright,
But thou who hold'st the rose, thou hast no right
About the sacred secret to converse.
The inmost thought no words can e'er reveal,
And truth must ever in some deep well lie ;
Read but the book the seven thunders seal,
Lest their dread utterance should rend the sky ;
Be mine the silver trump earth's hearts to reach,
Thy golden silence doth the angels teach.

III.

But when our hearts have found the one true way,
Then each shall clasp the rose with willing hand,
And thus 'fore God and holy angels stand,
And with our voices joined we'll praise and pray,
And tell the coming of the perfect day,
When one shall stand upon the sea and land
Declaring time no more; how solemn, grand,
The stone before death's door shall roll away.
Old things have passed away, all things are new;
A greater destiny to us is given;
Behold, O God, new earth! behold new heaven!
All things are good, all perfect in Thy view.
When souls with one accord sound octaves true,
That harmony includes the mystic seven!

IV.

THRICE thou hast called me, thrice I am thy queen;
And O, thrice queenly, love, I'll strive to be,
And with my sceptre rule the air and sea,
And bid glad earth put on her newest green.
For thee the moon shall shine with brighter sheen,
The stars shall bring thee blessed dreams of me.
Since I am queen I'll reign right royally,
And nought twixt thee and me shall intervene.
My empire now is thy unquestioning heart;
Put suns, and stars, and worlds i' the other side,
I would chose thee, thou art my counterpart,
And I, O love, I am thy queen, thy bride!
We two contain all life, the mystic scroll
Writ on two hearts we may at last unroll !

Song.

Thy spirit shines amid the stars,
  As white and bright as they,
It flames in the Aurora bars,
  It gleams in ocean spray;
My spirit sails the airy sea,
And finds alone its God and thee.

In the long watches of the night
  Thine arms are round me thrown,
And soul to soul in regions bright
  We sail, we two alone;
Immensity expressed in space,
Our Maker's soul shines through each face.

Through the white portal whence we came,
· We shall ascend again,
When we have shown the Living Name
  Unto the sons of men,
Then merged in thee, and thou in me,
We both shall sink in Deity.

Night Song.

Let thy soul melt in mine, that is love's sleeping,
Forget my own to smile, forget to weep ;
The One great Soul above His watch is keeping,
For He alone can slumber not nor sleep.

Rest, rest in Him, thus let our spirits slumber,
Forgetting earthly bliss and earthly pain ;
All love supreme, and joys no tongue can number,
Must melt at last to one, in One again.

Our souls had gained the heights of highest heaven,
Scaled the last arch that God set in the sky,
Then with electric force again were driven
Toward dark earth to bring light from on high.

And through the darkness still the great Ligh
    shineth—
The one true Light that we are set to keep ;
But O, for heavenly rest my spirit pineth,
When, my belovèd, shall He give us sleep ?

Interlude.

THE TEMPTATION.

I.

The love of all the women in the world
I think is blended in my love for thee.
As Cleopatra loved Marc Antony,
So might I love ; as toward dark hell was hurled
Francesca, Juliet in love's maelstrom whirled,
So by love's passion might I also be.
Let not thine eyes look so beseechingly,
Lest my hand drop the flag I have unfurled.
Yea, we could die, love, 'twere not hard to die,
Thy hand in mine pillowed upon thy breast ;
But having lost the earth, to lose the sky,
To see thine anguish e'en though unexpressed,
Ah, that were hell indeed ! yea, damned were I
If I could yield heaven's peace for earth's unrest.

II.

WHAT eye could guess thy great, warm passionate
    heart
Lay throbbing thus beneath its veil of snow ?
Ah, thou like me hast depths and depths below,
And know'st the whole of love, the ache, the smart,
The anguish, the desire ;—the counterpart
Of love celestial is earth's heart of woe,
And 'tis earth's discord, love, that pains us so ;
Yet here will I descend since here thou art.
Yea, we must know the whole of life's deep pain,
As we have known the whole of heavenly bliss,
Walk hand in hand through hell without one stain,
To lift this world from out the deep abyss
Into the light ; when Christ shall come again,
Let Him not find on earth a traitor's kiss.

III.

O THAT dark curse once laid upon Eve's head,
Still, still its shadow rests upon my brow
In spite of prayer, in spite of holy vow,
And with Thy blood, O Christ, my hands are red :
For me again the sacred drops are shed,
And crucified afresh I see Thee now !

Oh, let me bear the cross ; oh, let me bow,
The sin is mine, and all my glory fled.
And thou, O my belovèd, have I cast
The curse again upon the soul of thee ?
Oh have I fed thee from that damnèd tree
When thou hast trusted me ?   Too bright to last
Were those fair visions, all their radiance past ;
Behold thy sin doth find its roots in me.

IV.

O, LOVE, the bitter ache ! the bitter ache !
The woe of sin and of sin's banishment,
Our souls from light to outer darkness sent,
Because our earthly hands have dared to take
The fruit intended our souls' thirst to slake—
Because the tempter's voice with His was blent
So cunningly—until the dear voice went
Leaving the chaos that our sin doth make.
O my Redeemer, Christ, thou Crucified !
Is it in vain that Thy dear blood was shed ?
Is it for nought Thy sacred wounds have bled ?
And hast Thou lived, O God, and hast Thou died
Here on this earth below ?   Yea, Thou hast said,
Washed in Thy blood we may be purified.

" If we say that we have no sin we deceive ourselves, and the truth is not in us ; but if we confess our sins, God is faithful and just to forgive us our sins, and to cleanse us from all unrighteousness."   1 JOHN i. 8, 9.

Part IV.

THE TRIUMPH.

"The spiritual ministry of revived man extends to every phenomenon that can be manifested in nature."

SAINT-MARTIN.

O MY one love, my one, my only love,
My perfect soul, my strong free-hearted lover,
My pearl of price whom I at last discover,
Swift as an eagle, art thou calm as dove ?
And wouldst thou swiftly, calmly soar above
This earth ?   And soar with me, me and none other,
My king, my peer, my spouse, and my soul's
        brother ;
Equals we are, our matehood we shall prove.
My soul Thou hast redeemed and purified,
And Thou my body too shalt so redeem.
For Thou hast borne the cross, and crucified
Hast been, and from Thee holy light doth stream ;
The vital flood that issues from Thy side
Doth make the whole glad earth with life to teem.

The Sacred Rose.

BE as you were when first my heart did move
Toward you ; silent, repressed, or even cold.
Be as you were, true love is never bold,
But ever waiteth still its strength to prove.
A budding flower that never blooms is love,—
And thou this flower half-blown must ever hold ;
It will reveal itself then fold on fold,
And thou may'st see within the sacred Dove.
Seek not to hasten that pure holy hour,
Seek not to pluck unripe the fruit divine ;
Wait on the Lord I say, wait on His power,
It cannot fail as faileth mine and thine ;
O guard till then this ever-living flower,
That He unto our care doth now consign.

WHEN God speaks I will hear, but speak not thou ;
What God says I will do, let not thy will
Perplex me ; do not thou too my cup fill
With sorrow, but together let us bow,
The crown of thorns, if need be, on each brow ;
Let His dear voice the raging tempest still,
Then shall we feel the blest ecstatic thrill
That shall redeem from death and broken vow.

Henceforth let my desire be to my God ;
Let me gaze evermore toward His face,
So He but fill me with His heavenly grace,
I'll kneel and kiss the scourging, chastening rod ;
So He but bring me to His holy place,
I'll walk where ne'er a woman's foot hath trod.

Love's Gifts.

WHAT shall I give, O love, to thee ?
What shall I give thee, the air or sea?
I would make thee lord of the whole glad earth,
For that is thy right, thy portion by birth ;
If I am a queen, a king thou must be,
And rule thy kingdom as royally.

What can I give that thou hast not now ?
Vows may be broken, I will not vow ;
My soul is thine, and were sweet love slain,
My soul could call it to life again.
When I give thee my soul thou hast all, I trow,
That man can receive, or God allow.

Love Sleeping.

WE stood together, love, and side by side
We watched the face of our immortal child;
It lay so still it never moved or smiled,
And fear came on me lest sweet love had died,
I thought, "Must still the Spirit wait His bride?
And the sad earth, to heaven unreconciled,
Lose the sweet message of the Dove so mild,
And Christ though risen still be crucified?"
Then the voice said, "Love sleeps, it cannot die,
For born in heaven it must descend to earth
And dwell with men; whatever lives on high
Is wrought out here and has its earthly birth,
But keep ye pure as dwellers in the sky,
Your child shall then inherit God-like mirth"

"Pray for Me."

PRAY for thee, my beloved? Yea, will I
Pray at the dawn, when the first streaks of light
Proclaim God's will upon the face of night;
When the bright sun shoots upward through the sky,
And there reveals the will of God on high,
Will I too pray; and when those beams so bright
Are sunk behind the hills and lost to sight,
And when night's stars declare that He is nigh.

With all the pulses of my throbbing heart,
With every living breath I draw, I'll pray !
While seasons come and go and days depart,
Though worlds dissolve, and suns shall fade away,
While soul immortal lives, my life must be
One concentrated prayer, O love, for thee !

I SEE beyond thy face, beyond thine eyes,
Beyond the beauty of thine earthly form,
I see thy heavenly image in the skies,
Though still obscured by the dark clouds of storm :
And oh, I hunger for that soul of thine,
I long to eat with thee the holy bread,
And from thy hand to take the living wine,
The marriage feast when soul to soul is wed.
I long to stand with thee in Paradise
Beneath the tree, to hear the living voice
Say, " Ye are redeemed, redeemed, bought with a
        price,
Glad earth and sky together may rejoice ! "
Oh, Lord, my God, banish earth's sin and pain,
Grant that we may our Paradise regain.

THESE lines I write are writ for every one
Whose heart hath loved, and loving sufferèd;
And those in whom love's pain—dark sin—hath bred,
And those whose hearts by sin are turned to stone,
And for all hungering hearts that ache alone,
And poor stained hearts whence love hath almost
    fled,
And burning hearts who, crucified, have bled—
I too have suffered all that these have known.
Yea, sin, and pain, and woe, and misery,
Torture, and shame, and anguish, and desire—
My blood is red as theirs, and throbbed through me
As fiercely, until cleansed by heavenly fire;
Now truth's sweet comforting hath set me free,
I fain would make all earth to heaven aspire.

Song.

PEACE, peace on earth, good will to men,
Sing the old song again, again ;
Peace, peace on earth, and joy on high,
The angel choir is drawing nigh.

O hast thou heard the heavenly strain ;
And heard responsive earth's refrain ?
O, Christ shall come—He draweth nigh :
Behold the day spring from on high !

"God's Gift to Me."

God's gift to thee ?
   Yea, love, God-sent
Since thou dost see
   I rest content,
Nor shade of fear
Can me come near
 . If I with Him am blent.

If thou canst see
    That 'tis His will
Gives me to thee,
    And holds me still ;
If in my face
Thou seest His grace
I may thy prayers fulfil.

Whate'er I be,
    It 'tis His power
Sends me to thee ;
    Then richest dower
I am indeed,
And thy heart's need
Shall bless my natal hour.

'Tis blest to be
    God's messenger,
By His decree
    Love to confer ;
Thus in thine eyes
I shall be wise,
And in no thing can err.

His eye can see
　　Thy inmost soul,
And guiding me,
　　Can yield the whole
Of that pure love
Which born above
Must now our lives control.

In purity
　　This love expressed,
Security
　　Dwells in each breast,
And thus we stand
While hand clasps hand,
And heart to heart is pressed.

The mystic Three
　　Are blent in One,
The Unity,
　　God, Spirit, Son,
The waters shine
The bread, the wine
Declare His will is done.

Emanation.

Out of the depths of the Infinite Being eternal,
Out of the cloud more bright than the brightness of
          sun,
Out of the inmost the essence of spirit supernal,
          We issued as one.

First essence electric, concentric, revolving, subduing,
We throbbed through the ether, a part of the infinite
          germ,
Dissolving, resolving, absorbing, reforming, renewing,
          The endless in term.

Through forms multifarious onward and ever ad-
          vancing,
Progressing through ether from molecule to planet
          and star,
Forms infinitesimal revealed by the sunbeam while
          dancing,
          Controlled from afar.

Then part of the elements swayed by invisible forces,
The spirit of flame interchangeably water and air,
And matter more gross, still moulded by stars in
          their courses,
          To forms new and rare.

Part of the salt of the sea—of the fathomless ocean—
Part of the growth of the earth, and the light hid
      within,
The Boundless and Endless revealed in each varying
      motion
      Unknown yet to sin.

The breath of all life, harmonious, ductile, complying,
Obedient lapsed in the force of the Infinite Will,
Untiring, unresting, incessant, unknowing, undying,
      Love's law we fulfil.

Spirit of growth in the rocks, and the ferns, and the
      mosses,
Spirit of growth in the trees, and the grasses, and
      flowers,
Rejoicing in life, unconscious of changes or losses,
      Of days or of hours.

Spirit of growth in the bird and the bee, ever tending
To form more complex its beauty and use thus com-
      bined,
Adapted perfection, the finite and infinite blending,
      One gleam from One Mind.

Thus spirally upward we come from the depths of
  creation,
The man and the woman—the garden of Eden have
  found,
And joined by the Lord in an endless and holy
  relation
   Ensphered and made round.

The innermost law of their being fulfilling, obeying,
The King and the Queen, perfected, companioned,
  are crowned,
The Incomprehensible thus in expression conveying
   Its ultimate bound.

Obedience still is the law of each fresh emanation,
The prayer to the Father, "Not my will, but Thy
  will be done,"
Then deathless, immortal, we pass through all forms
  of creation,
   The twain lost in One.

I WOULD that I might marry my sweet thought
To words that should convey the soul of sense,
Clothe it with language pure, sublime, intense,
And wondrous rhythm with such meaning fraught,
That every ear might hear, and by it taught,
Pierce through these Babel clouds, so thick and
    dense,
That hide us each from each ; and thus commence
New life in love, where discords melt to naught.
Mankind is of one blood, one soul, one mind :
O hearts clasp hands, see yourselves in each other,
Give love for hate, live out the gospel kind,
And soon shall each dread foe become a brother ;
Yea, ye are brothers now, but O so blind ;
Can ye not see our one great common Mother ?

" Love is an expansion, not a contraction, a giving. not a
craving : it breaks in pieces the condensing circle of self,
and goes forth in the delightfulness of its desire to bless."
History of Henry Earl of Moreland, the Fool of Quality.

THOU art my centre, love, and thence from thee
My love doth spread itself o'er the wide earth ;
My spirit travaileth to give new birth
To light : to lift and let the oppressed go free ;
Draw all their sins and sorrows unto me,
And suffer once for all, to give them mirth
For tears ; to feed the hungry hearts ; for dearth,
Plenty and riches—faith and charity.
Hope is the star that leads us on our way,
Faith is the evidence of things unseen,
And by this evidence we all may say
That nought with God is common or unclean,
Then charity is born of faith's pure ray,
And Christ shall all the golden harvest glean.

Interlude.

THE TENOR VOICE.

An Answer.

WHAT matters, love, if eyes be dark or blue,
Hazel, or black, or violet, or gray?
It only matters what the dear eyes say,
And if their gaze be earnest, steadfast, true.
I love your eyes because your soul looks through;
I see beyond their depths, and far away
In some bright region where pure spirits stray,
And in your eyes I catch some glimpse of you.
Are they not dear?   Yea, dearer than the stars,
Loadstars to me, shining through darkest night
Radiant with love, intense with spirit light,
Fitful and changing as the fires of Mars,
And luminous as bright Aurora bars:
Would they might shine for ever in my sight!

A Request.

THINK of me, dearest, let thy thoughts entwine
About my life as tendrils hold the flowers ;
O think of me in all thy waking hours.
I have not any love, O love, but thine,
How could I dream that such love could be mine,
Who never sought to win it ? by what powers
Have I enchained thee ? what strange fate endowers
Me with thyself, the soul for which I pine ?
I only feared to mar thy peaceful life ;
I held aloof lest I should stain or blot
Thy pure white soul which hath nor shade nor spot,
I kept my love afar, and that love's strife ;
God tried my faith, but now withholds the knife,
And what He gives, I take, and question not.

Self-Abnegation.

No man can yield himself more utterly
Than I have yielded; dear one, work thy will,
I have not any choice but to fulfil
The sweet commands that thou hast laid on me.
It were most sweet to let me die for thee—
A living death I die, if love could kill—
Love shall destroy all power to work thee ill,
Thou art my queen, and I must bow the knee.
Rule me by right divine, my blessèd one,
The sceptre of thy womanhood, God-given,
Shall guide me here, and point the way to heaven;
I'll kneel with thee and say, " His will be done !."
My life anew in thee I have begun,
Thou hast infilled me with the sacred leaven.

Thou shalt be free, yea, love, as free as air,
As free as love itself that by restraint
Must die; thou shalt not hear my heart's complaint;
I won thee freely, and shall I not dare
To freely hold ?   What joy could e'er compare
To this—receiving more than wish could paint
Or fancy picture ?   O, my dove ! my saint !
Could inward vision yearn for sight more rare ?
I yield to thee my all, my life, my soul,
Knowing full well thou wilt not fail to keep
My happiness as thine.   Ah, let me sleep
Here on thy breast where I have lain the whole
Of all I am, or may be—if thou toll
My death-knell, be it so, *thou* shalt not weep.

The Thread Resumed.

" THE King can do no wrong," and thou, *my* King,
Art right.—My own, in thee I put my trust,
Thy love my treasure, which nor moth nor rust
Can e'er consume ; my rock to which I cling,
Let storm-birds cry, or the wild tempests fling
Their wrath upon us ; old worlds melt to dust,
We shall remain as conquerors—we thrust,
Time forward, knowing all that Time shall bring.
By right divine, ruling by laws of spirit
The powers that be ; their little transient hour
Must melt by force of the incoming power ;
Soon shall the blessed meek the earth inherit ;
The peacemakers shall then receive their merit,
When Christ shall come and bring to each his dower.

A Wish.

I WOULD be like a rose
That blossoms in the wilderness,
Giving my fragrance to the air,
My heart to my belovèd.

Song.

O LORD, make sacred my love to my love,
It is Thou who hast made him so sweet to see,
It is Thou who hast made him so dear to me,
And methought as he held me I saw the Dove
Brooding in hallowed light above,
And I heard the voice as of Deity.

Flêche d'Amour.

WHEN God doth call me, I must go
To heights of bliss, or depths of woe,
And which it be I may not know ;
　　　　I only follow !

The love He gives me I must take
And cherish it for His dear sake ;
Though rankling wounds the love shafts make,
　　　　I needs must follow !

O'er stony ways with bleeding feet,
Through meadows green and blossoms sweet,
Through flood and fire, through blinding sleet,
　　　　I still must follow !

My heart, though arrow-pierced, I wear,
Its life-blood, drop by drop, I dare
Let flow, its burning still must bear
    And only follow !

I may not turn to left or right,
I may not stop for day or night,
With eyes still fixed on love's clear light,
    I ever follow !

Two friends do bear me company,
And walk on either side of me,
With sleep and death I still am free,
    For they too follow !

And when I cry for stress of pain,
Sweet sleep doth bind my wounds again,
And in his strengthening arms I'm lain,
    And dreaming follow !

And when I have no strength to cry,
And turn to death with piteous eye,
He saith, " When love fails, here am I,"
    I ever follow !

O I HAVE thee, what could I want beside ?
In thy deep being doth all beauty hide,
And one by one each rare and radiant gem
Plucked from thy heart shines in my diadem.
Lo ! now a pearl whose iridescence fair
Gleams like pale moonlight in my woven hair,
And now a ruby in whose depths repose
The hidden meanings of the sacred rose,
The lustrous purple bloom of amethyst,
Where righteousness and peace have met and kissed.
Yea, all the hidden treasures of the earth
Are brought to light in thee, and have new birth,
Thou art the man that seers of old beheld ;
A Prince of Peace, for in thy heart is quelled
All discords, and the kingdom of thy soul
Is ruled by Christ, bowing to His control.
He is indeed thy great, thy elder Brother,
And thou art part of Him ; the holy mother
Hath given new birth to thee, and set thee free,
No longer earthbound, part of Deity.
Crowned with the light and glory of the sun,
Its radiance thine, and with thy nature one.

The universal essence welds and mates
All heavenly souls, and rules inferior fates,
The earth-born ties are snapt as with a sword,
And soul to soul is joined by word of God,
And whom He joins, no man can put asunder,
The still small voice repeals the earthly thunder !

Song.

WHAT is the sum of our lives,
    As we two journey along ?
What is the sum of our lives,
    Flowers and rhythm and song ?
Strew we the pathway for others ?
Songs that are prayers for our brothers ?
    Help for the weak from the strong !

As we two journey along,
    Pale sorrow droops and death flies ;
Love blossoms forth as a song,
    Peace and protection arise ;
Blessings to children and mothers,
Fathers and maidens and brothers
    Echo love's praise to the skies !

Song.

BROTHER and sister are we,
By some strange olden decree
Thy sister am I, and thy spouse.
Lo ! the halo that circles our brows
Makes us one in divine mystery.

I.

O MY divinest one, what have I done,
What am I, to be part of thine and thee ?
Thou art large hearted ; like the rhythmëd sea
Thy nature compasseth each clime and zone.
What am I to thee ? thou dost stand alone,
Perfect, self-centred, poised, controlled, yet free,
Godlike in power, conscious of Deity,
Immovable as God's first corner stone.
Can I be equal ?   Sister, queen, and bride ?
Then must my heart embrace the living whole,
Centre, circumference, girdle pole to pole
With sympathies as deep and broad and wide
As thine ; yea, one with thee !   Ah, side by side
A peerless pearl ! a universal soul !

II.

When thou withdrawest thy outer self from sight,
I see the inner beauty of thy soul ;
As when the sun withdraws and shows the night
Where starry clusters gleam and planets roll.
These days and nights of present-absent love
Are but as hours in our one perfect day ;
We dwell in endless light beyond, above,
In fields Elysian do our spirits stray.
Far from the knowledge of this ill or good
We pluck the living fruit from living trees,
And feed each other with supernal food,
Within the presence of the Eye that sees !
Would the sad earth might taste that bread divine,
And know the ecstacy of living wine.

III.

I think our bodies are too weak to bear
The full and perfect bliss of our strong souls ;
I think some gentler will suspends, controls
The vital power that hovereth in the air ;
Our spirits soar and climb, but scarcely dare
To call down thunder; how it groans and rolls,
Vibrates and swells, as some great bell that tolls,

Muffled and distant.   What doth it declare ?
Death unto death, and life to the new life—
The curse removed, freedom from all our sin,
The word revealed, buried so long within,
The hand restrained from sacrificial knife
Through Abraham's faith—sweet peace controlling
    strife,
The Sabbath-day of rest that all shall win.

IV.

I SEE thee now in all bright living things,
I stand no more alone beneath the sky,
And every moment on swift silent wings
Whispers my heart that thy deep soul is nigh.
Thy love is borne to me in waves of air,
And bathes me in soft oceans of delight ;
I float I know not how, I care not where,
Lost in thy love I feel nor day nor night.
The murmurs of the solemn-voicèd sea,
The crimson purple rift where sun went down.
Are but as tokens of thy love to me ;
In all sweet things thy tenderness is shown ;
The fresh spring daisies smiling at my feet
Express thy smiles, and thy loved words repeat.

Venus Victrix.

O DOST thou see me in the morn ?
  And in the violet's eye ?
A goddess of the seafoam born
  Am I, and of the sky.
Canst thou not find me in the air ?
Then, love, I am not anywhere.

The flowers shall show thee where my feet
  Have been ; the air's caress,
That fans thy cheek with odours sweet,
  Is but my wind-blown tress ;
That purple gloom in sunset skies
Is but the shadow of mine eyes.

Sometimes an earthly form I wear,
  As woman I am seen,
But thy love-lighted eyes declare
  That I am goddess-queen ;
And being queen of thy dear heart,
I rule all things of thee a part.

H

Come night !   Come Romeo !   Come thou day in night,
For thou wilt lie upon the wings of night
Whiter than new snow on a raven's back.
Come gentle night !   Come loving black browed night,
Give me my Romeo ! and when he shall die
Take him and cut him out in little stars ;
And he will make the face of heaven so fine
That all the world will be in love with night,
And pay no worship to the garish sun.

Romeo and Juliet. Shakspeare. Act III. Scene II.

Song.

THE fair day dies, the fairer night advances ;
Move swift ye tardy hours on golden wings,
Come, darkling night, begin your starry dances,
My pulses beat in time, my heart's-blood sings.

Shine on, thou evening star, thou shalt discover
And lead my loved one here unto my feet,
Then the broad wings of night shall brood and hover·
O'er the white soul of him my soul shall greet.

Look down, ye clustered stars, ye hosts of heaven,
For in his eyes doth shine as pure a light,
What wonder when such stars to me are given
That I forget the day and worship night?

I.

Thou art afar beside the lonely sea,
And I amid the city's busy throng;
Thou art afar, but yet I hear the song
That thy heart sings in solemn ecstasy;
My heart doth throb in unison with thee,
The sea and night have made my soul grow strong,
Strong for the conflict, strong to meet all wrong
With one great burst of golden harmony.
Thy spirit draws me and I gladly fly
Unto thee, love, forgetting earthly pain —
The body's absence is the spirit's gain —
For thus apart our souls must draw more nigh
And soar together upward, till on high
We both shall hear once more the heavenly strain.

II.

Thou should'st be here, O love! thou should'st be
    here !
The swift blood mounts my heart and then retreats;
Can words translate the rhythm of heart-beats ?
Can my soul's thirst call thy dear soul more near ?

H 2

O to my waiting eyes could'st thou appear !
What joy ! what rapture ! when thy spirit greets
Its inner self, my song thy heart repeats,
And both our beings blend in one bright sphere.
We do defy the bonds of time and space,
For we have entered our eternal rest,
All nature seems a pageant where thy grace
In myriad forms and wonders is expressed ;
The shining stars reveal thy blessed face,
And O, my heaven lies hid within thy breast.

Morning.

Out of deep slumber and Lethe-like sleep and forget-
    ting,
I wake ; the new day has bathed the broad earth
    with its light;
Gone are the shadows and clouds and the heart's
    vain regretting,
Borne far away on the wings of the sweet soothing
    night.

I wake to new day, new light, and new love in its
    dawning,
Yet the sun is the same that has shone since creation
    begun,
And thou, O my soul! when thou comest 'tis ever
    love's morning,
And I drink deep of life from thy beams, O my glory!
    my sun!

Clothe me with light, and wrap all thy colours around
    me,
The gold and the purple, the crimson, and scarlet,
    and green,
With the soft pearly tints of the dove and the azure
    surround me,
Thus clothed with thy love I shall walk the glad
    earth as a queen.

O heart of my heart, when our sun for the last time
    is setting,
We shall wander again in the regions of bliss and of
    light,
Face to face evermore we shall know neither sleep
    nor forgetting,
For the one golden day of our love hath no shadow
    nor night.

Now though the clouds and the darkness of earth
  hover o'er us,
Now though the gloom has eclipsed the full light
  that we own,
The pillar of cloud and of fire travels ever before us,
Our footsteps are guided and watched from the height
  of the throne.

God's children are we, new-born from the heart of
  the Mother,
Baptized with the water, the Spirit, and heavenly fire,
We are one thus in Christ; re-risen in Him—Elder
  Brother,
Our sins died with Thee, and with Thee shall our
  souls too aspire.

We rule in Thy kingdom with Thee, for the vision
  hath taught us
That peace is the prophet preparing the way of the
  Lord,
And Thou with thy blood hast redeemed us, O
  Brother, and bought us,
And at Thy command earth shall sheathe her swift
  severing sword.

Night.

Thou sleepest while I wake, but O above thee
  My spirit broods ; ah sleep, belovèd, sleep
A dreamless deep repose ; yea, I who love thee
  Bid thee sleep on, lest thou should'st wake and
    weep.

Dear heart, that long hast borne the weight of sorrow,
  How wilt thou bear the greater weight of joy—
The heightened bliss that gains with each to-morrow
  The gold of life unmixed with base alloy ?

How wilt thou dare to seek the hidden treasure ?
  How wilt thou dare to hear the Word revealed ?
O love, the countless joys beyond all measure,
  The mystery that buried ages sealed ?

At last we stand together at the portal,
  At last we dare to ope the golden gate ;
Lo ! my belovèd, see the fruit immortal
  Ripe for the plucking ; shall we longer wait ?

As gods we stand unknown to sin or sorrow,
  Our mortal life is dead, our mortal pain,
No yesterday, and no to-day nor morrow,
  Our lost eternity we shall regain.

Lo ! in a moment all is spread before us—
   All that has been, and is, and is to be—
We sound the word and heavenly hosts adore us,
   We throb in unison with Deity.

The magical, the mystic word, the number
   That holds the secret of the inner life,
Creation wakes as from a long deep slumber,
   And peace and plenty banish dearth and strife.

I.

O Lord, my human words are all too weak
To tell the love my heart for him doth bear ;
But O, my Father, wilt thou not declare
And let the harmonies of heaven speak ?
My heart's great love as great a voice doth seek,
But though I gained the thunders of the air
He would not heed unless Thy word were there,
So blessed is my love, so pure and meek.
I cannot tell him, no, I have no way
To show him all the heights and depths of love,
I can but mutely stand, and trusting pray
That He who sent this blessing from above
Will fill my loved one's heart by night and day
With heavenly murmurs of the brooding Dove.

II.

I SOUGHT my love at night in a dark wood
Where flitting shades and shadowy phantoms flee,
And there on every side they beckoned me,
And when I followed, they in taunting mood
Cried, " Is thy lover fair, or is he good ? "
Their faces leered and peered from every tree,
And all was blinding chance and mockery,
And I, heart-weary, pale and weeping stood.
I sank upon the ground and wept, and wept ;
My love, my own true love had failed me there,
And overcome at length I weeping slept,
And sleeping, weeping, murmured many a prayer ;
When lo ! from my own heart my loved one crept
And bore me in his arms to upper air.

"I will sing a new song which resounds in my breast."

The Magic Bark.

BUILD me a bark, love, that we may sail
    Over the seas to the Islands of Light;
Build me a bark that shall stand every gale,
    Swift as a white-winged bird in its flight;
        Love, let us sail!

Strong slender masts of the tall northern trees,
    White curving sails blown out by the wind,
Cleaving the tempest a bright bird that flees,
    And leaves the old world and its darkness behind,
        And sails with love's breeze!

Free as the ocean, we know not nor care
    Whither, for somewhere the new country lies
Waiting our coming, a continent fair,
    Whose plains, hills, and rivers shall greet our
        glad eyes.
        Salt winds, blow us there!

The new land of freedom, the birthplace of song,
   Where the weak may find shelter, the weary find
      rest,
Where new lusty life replaces old wrong,
   And the joy of creation makes labour seem blest,
     The salt wind blows strong !

We stand once again 'neath the old virgin trees,
   We watch the Aurora's bright gleams of strange
      light ;
The long grasses wave on the wide prairie seas,
   The old earth beneath, and above broods the night,
     Blow, blow, southern breeze !

O Nature ! our Mother, we rocked on thy breast,
   Have found the lost secret that all men may win,
The fountain of life, and the garden of rest ;
   We banish the curse when we banish our sin :
     Blow, blow, breezes blest !

Our feet to the earth, and our souls to the skies
   Primeval, co-equal, eternal we stand,
The truths of all ages lie hid in thine eyes,
   And heaven's between us when hand claspeth hand.
     O south wind, arise !

Blow winds from the east, or blow winds from the
    west,
    Come day or come night, and the seasons that
      change,
The spring brings the leaf, and the bird builds her
    nest,
    The new waxes old, and the old waxes strange,
        But all winds blow rest !

Yea, rest to the hearts that have drunk deep of love,
    When the twain halves are melted in circles com-
      plete,
And ascend in a widening spiral ; the Dove
    Doth descend upon them, and earth heaven doth
      greet,
        Blow, winds from above !

"I know that whatsoever God doeth, it shall be for ever ;
nothing can be put to it, nor anything taken from it : and
God doeth it that men should fear before Him."
ECCLESIASTES iii. 14.

Interlude.

ECHOES.

Song.

THREE things I shall praise God for when I'm dying,
Remembering how love His law fulfils :—
For the soft wind that through my lattice sighing
Brings me the cooing sound of birdlings' trills,
The light grown strong behind the distant hills,
And in my arms my own beloved one lying !

The Mirror.

A RADIANT mirror I would be,
Within whose depths my love might see
The perfect beauties of his soul
Reflected there complete and whole,
And learn by looking in my face,
To know his spirit's inner grace.

Parted.

By night upon my bed the tear-drops flow;
Two things I long for—death, and thy embrace
Only to feel thy kisses on my face,
Only to see thee, dear one, e'er I go
Beyond the reach of earth's great bliss or woe:
Yea, thou shalt follow to my hiding place,
We both shall find through His abiding grace
The garden where eternal roses blow.
As thou hast drawn me earthward by thy love,
And I have shared all mortal pangs with thee,
So shall thy soul seek mine in realms above,
And thou shalt share the joys of heaven with me;
Lo, now I see the white wings of the Dove!
Ah, loose the cord, and set my spirit free!

Song.

Love, Love, sweet Love, I know not what to say
In praise of thee ; I know not what thou art,
A holy flower that blooms in paradise,
A crystal tear that flows from starlike eyes,
Sweet peace serene that dwells within the heart—
The calm of night, the gladness of the day !

Love, Love, sweet Love, ah, tell me what thou art,
Why dwellest thou within my loved one's eyes,
Those twin-like stars that turn my night to day ?
Why dost thou pierce my soul with that bright ray
That seems a gleam shot out from Paradise ?
Canst thou not still the throbbing of my heart ?

Love, Love, sweet Love, a flower of Paradise,
Eternal Spring born of an endless day,
I may not know thee yet, nor all thou art,
But lighten thou the darkness of my heart,
And breathe thy music through each word I say,
That I may still find favour in his eyes.

I

Retrogression.

Go from me if thou wilt, thou canst not find
Another love like mine, though thou should'st see
All earth's fair faces ; they would only be
As fragments to thee, though all womankind
Sue for thy love ; from henceforth thou art blind,
I am thy sight, thou drawest thy light from me—
The rising sun of thy eternity,
Pulse to thy heart, and magnet to thy mind.
Pluck myriad flowers from each successive Spring,
They will not make thee love the Spring the less,
Rather their odours to thy sense will bring
Repeated proof of Spring's sweet loveliness.
To thee henceforth all birds will ever sing
My song, all nature will my love express.

Initiation.

Good-bye ! good-bye ! my bark puts out to sea ;
  Good-bye, old friends, good-bye my native shore,
The cable's cut, my earth-bound soul is free,
  The airy heights are gained for evermore.

The past drops from me as a robe outworn,
  Things that I knew I shall not know again,
Into new life my radiant soul is born,
  And walks a spirit midst the sons of men.

The flowers of earth I plucked with eager hands,
  And ripened fruits I gladly now resign ;
My soul with peerless jewels crownèd stands,
  And all earth's wealth of hidden treasures mine.

No more the weary heartache, nor the tears,
  No more the doubt and blindness of despair,
Mine eyes are opened, and the inner spheres
  Reveal immortal fruits and flowers most rare.

The centred soul sits free upon a throne,
  And penetrates illimitable space,
And binds all nature, yet it is alone,
  Eternally unfolding inner grace.

Upon my heart engraved the holy law,
  By which God made the world and called it good;
The word of love and fear, which prophets saw
  In fragments, now is joined and understood.

The future lives enfolded in the past,
  The present is a type of what shall be ;
The seamless garment shall be ours at last,
  And death be swallowed up in victory.

Keep thou the saying of the Lord, and live
  For ever in the love to God and man,
And thou shalt find more blessed 'tis to give
  Than to receive; then shalt thou see the plan

Of universal love throughout all space,·
  Working salvation to the souls of men—
Then Paradise shall be thy dwelling place,
  And thou shalt eat the living fruit again.

Song.

Shut not the gates of thy soul to me !
   O love, my love, I would fain abide
Where the river floweth silently
   'Tween the living trees on its either side ;
Let me not dwell in the outer night,
I long to bathe in thy holy light.

Open the gates of thy soul to me,
   O love, my love, let my spirit hide,
And lose itself in the Holy Three,
   The Bridegroom waits for His mystic Bride,
Away from the day, away from the night,
Bathing for ever in holy light.

Resignation.

I DO not ask Thee, Lord, to give
   My love to me,
I only ask that he may live,
   O Lord, in Thee.

I do not ask that I may see
   My loved one's face,
I only pray that he may be
   Filled with Thy grace.

No more I ask Thee, Lord, to show
   This love of mine,
I only pray that he may know
   Thy love divine.

Part V.

VALEDICTION.

I.

God, who hath made us one, hath made us twain ;
Sundered on earth, in heaven we are united ;
Celestial bliss is born of earthly pain,
Eternity restores what time hath blighted.
Love's body hath been slain by cruel chance,
But still its spirit lives, and shall arise
Freed from the chains of time and circumstance,
And lift our hearts again to bluest skies.
For thee I leave all outward things behind,
For thee I lay my earth-born body down,
So I may once again thy spirit find,
And hold and claim thee as my very own.
All clouds between us twain must soon disperse,
Our souls the heavenly marriage shall rehearse.

II.

THEE have I found again whom I had lost;
Within thy heart once more my heart reposes;
Alas! alas! we have been tempest-tossed,
But now my spirit's life thy life encloses.
I am thy centre, and circumference,
An atmosphere within, and all around thee,
I penetrate thy soul and every sense
Yields to my will which now again has bound thee;
Yea, thou art mine, the twain are lost in one,
The image of the Lord impressed in beauty,
By our submission His will shall be done,
And here below fulfilled the higher duty;
Our love shall fructify the barren earth,
And nature through our pangs receive new birth.

" My beloved spake, and said unto me, Rise up, my love, my fair one, and come away.

" For, lo, the winter is past, the rain is over and gone ;

" The flowers appear on the earth ; the time of the singing of birds is come, and the voice of the turtle is heard in our land.

" My beloved is mine, and I am his : he feedeth among the lilies.

" Awake, O north wind ; and come thou south ; blow upon my garden, that the spices thereof may flow out. Let my beloved come into his garden, and eat his pleasant fruits.

" My beloved is white and ruddy, the chiefest among ten thousand.

"Make haste, my beloved, and be thou like to a roe or to a young hart upon the mountains of spices."

SONG OF SOLOMON.

Spring Song.

THE sun so brightly shines to-day ;
   It is earth's bridal morn,
And all sweet nature seems to say,
   'Tis blessed to be born.
Arise, my love, and flee away,
   Nothing should be forlorn.

The winter's snows and frosts are past,
    The turtle's voice is heard
In all the land, and O, at last
    I too may call my bird;
And wilt not thou, my dove, fly fast
    To greet the welcome word?

The winter's gone, the woods are green,
    The tender flowers appear
To deck the earth, a gracious queen
    Whose kingly spouse is near;
O let thy face, my own, be seen,
    Thy voice, O let me hear!

My best belovèd one is mine,
    And I am his alone;
His love is better far than wine,
    His face as Lebanon—
Most excellent—as gold most fine—
    His head, my blessèd one.

Awake! awake! O northern wind,
    O south wind, rise and blow
Until my love his garden find,
    Where all sweet spices grow,
And pleasant fruits of every kind,
    And living waters flow.

Among ten thousand chief is he,
　　Is he whom my soul loves,
His face is as the cedar tree,
　　His eyes as eyes of doves ;
Yea, altogether fair to see,
　　His voice my being moves.

His mouth, O daughters, is most sweet—
　　My love is white and red ;
Upon the hills his blessed feet
　　Like hart or roebuck tread ;
Behold, he cometh skipping fleet :
　　Yea, come, as I have said !

I WOULD not win thee back to earthly things,
My best belovèd; if thy holy heart
Be not borne to me on the silent wings
Of faith, O then we must remain apart
A little longer: I will stand and wait
Beside the gulf that separates us twain,
Until I conquer Time and Death and Fate,
And bring thy spirit back to life again.
O thou, my chosen one, that heart of thine
Hath led me on the way that I have trod;
Thy hand hath plucked for me the fruit divine,
And in thy soul I read the laws of God.
O may not I illumine thy dark night,
And bring thee back to hope, to love, to light?

Song.

O LIFE! O joy! O love!
What more has Time to prove,
Now that my love and I
Are one eternally?
Now we can soar above,
Upward together fly,
And bid the world good-bye!

I MAY not see thy face, ah, nevermore
Behold thine eyes—twin shadows of the day,
Nor hear thy voice upon earth's barren shore,
My love, my love, now lost, far, far away,
And yet for me no sun shall ever rise,
No bird shall sing, no flower shall ever bloom;
But I shall feel thy presence in the skies
As light that pierces through the silent gloom.
For in the world within thou'rt ever there,
I find thee in the garden with my God,
Thy form immortal dwells within the air,
Thy hidden love upspringeth from the sod.
O that thine eyes that world of light might see,
That thou might'st find thy soul's eternity.

I WONDER love, shall we forget this earth
When we have gained once more the starry heights ?
Forget its pains we may, but its delights ?
O shall we not again long for new birth?
To share once more all mortal pangs and mirth,
The changing seasons, and the days and nights
Of aching love, which love alone requites,
The harvest's fulness, and the winter's dearth ?
What happy hours we passed beside the sea
Watching the white waves rolling to the shore,
Dashing amidst the foam as wild and free
As birds ; or listening to the ocean's roar,
Chanting our own heart's song of ecstasy—
Canst thou forget those happy days of yore ?

Nay, nay, the memory of all sweet things
I think will mingle with our heavenly bliss.
The joys above perchance consist of this—
Remembrance which for ever to us brings
The soul of sense ; leaving behind the stings
Of death and sin, sunk in the deep abyss.
Thou gav'st to me, O love, with thy one kiss,
The power to scale all heights with airy wings.
Methought the sleep of an eternal rest
With thee were all the joy that I could know,
But now methinks eternal waking best,
Or else to dream of joys known here below :
Can life yield aught to us more pure, more blest,
Than the deep peace of love without love's woe ?

Song.

I WOULD that thou might'st be born again,
    Dear one, born of the air and sea,
That thou might'st forget all the earth's deep pain,
    And lose thyself in the soul of me,
Wrapped soft around in a strange bright light,
Piercing the air in our rapid flight.

I would that thou might'st be born again,
    Sweetheart, born to thy liberty,
Then might thine ear hear the holy strain
    Sung by the angels for souls set free,
Then might'st thou pass in thy rapid flight,
Into the realms of eternal light.

WHY should we fear ?   Do the stars fear to shine?
The winds to blow, or the wild waves to roar?
Why should we fear ?   Is not our love divine?
Are not our spirits one for evermore ?
Nothing can touch us now but doubt or fear,
And perfect love should cast these both away,
All doors are open to our vision clear,
We bask for ever in eternal day.
Beyond the reach of Time or Death or Fate,
Into the region of pure conscious will,
Unto the *One* all things we consecrate,
His love we publish, and His laws fulfil ;
Time for a season still may blind thine eyes,
But thou with me shalt yet regain the skies.

Song.

THY soul hath brought me to my God,
   I have found Him in finding thee,
Before I knelt beneath His rod,
   But now His love alone I see.

Earth holds me not ; in Paradise
   I dwell for ever ; hear the voice
That spake of old and made men wise ;
   Who hath true wisdom may rejoice.

And all my ways are full of peace,
   My heart is one with God and thee,
And still must thankfulness increase,
   Till life one hymn of praise shall be.

"But she needed not to go to heaven, since heaven was ever in her and round about her, and that she could no more move from it than she could move from herself."

History of Henry Earl of Moreland, the Fool of Quality.

I.

WOULD I had been more tender, sweet, and true,
More pure, more noble, loving, more divine ;
Would that I might stand perfect in thy view,
As some sweet saint enclosed in holy shrine.
O thou must look beyond my human face
Into my inmost soul, and finding there
The temple of the Lord, and dwelling place
Of Holy Spirit, thou wilt not despair.
Then shalt thou see me as I was of old,
Yea, love, and as I shall be once again,
Filled with pure light and virtues manifold,
Revealed to thee and to the eyes of men.
O let this veil of flesh be rent in twain !
Heed not, O God, my cries of mortal pain !

II.

My heart doth know full well why love is blind,
It is that inner eyes may clearer see.
He closes outer sense that he may find
The essence and the soul of unity.
But thou, dear heart, art blinded by despair,
Which worketh sad division 'twixt us twain ;
Thy spirit eyes have lost the vision fair,
And nought canst thou discern but grief and pain.
Earth is a prison to thee ; thy soul groans
At being slave to earthly shows of things ;
In silent anguish thy poor spirit moans
And vainly tries to lift its fettered wings.
Alas ! that I these terrors clearly see,
Yet may not come to help or strengthen thee !

A Pilgrimage.

I.

Now will I go and walk the wide earth round,
And tell to every soul that I do meet,
The only way that true love may be found,
And how when found of all things good and sweet
It is most blest, most holy, most divine ;
It is the marriage feast of our dear Lord,
And He Himself will bless the bread and wine
For those two souls who are of one accord :
And how when God declares two spirits one,
That inmost heaven to them is then revealed,
They see what has been, is, and shall be done,
The mysteries to them are all unsealed.
And as they gaze on Him with rapturous eyes,
He leads them gently into Paradise.

II.

For my poor love I pray by night and day,
That from his woes he may obtain release,
Would I might bear his cross and give him peace!
I marvel much that he can find no way—
No light—no hope.   I know not what to say,
So silence keep, lest vain words should increase
The distance 'tween us; would his griefs might
      cease!
I love him so, yet nought can do but pray.
I feel with him his grievous misery,
His weight of woe, too heavy to be borne;
And yet in Spring such joy doth come to me
With all sweet growing things, I cannot mourn.
Strange that a double life within should be,
One heart filled with pure peace, and one forlorn.

III.

STRANGE, strange is life, most strange, yet I'm content
With my poor life imperfect though it be ;
I cannot but believe each thing is sent
By highest love ; God is my destiny,
He hath within my heart placed holy love,
And yet hath fettered me with human law,
As if by that the strength of love to prove,
To make it sacred, pure, without one flaw.
I think my heart could scarcely bear its pains
Did I not feel it is the hand of God
That scourges me, and thus my spirit gains
True strength to bow beneath the chastening rod.
Sweet soul who readest this, have charity,
For I do suffer for myself and thee.

IV.

YEA, let all lovers true round the wide earth
Grieve with my grief, and gladden with my joy;
For bitter tears I wept to give them mirth,
And purified my gold from base alloy.
And all my heart's wealth, see, I now pour forth—
My spices grown in the enchanted isles,
My mandates flash from the magnetic north,
And all the earth grows green beneath my smiles:
My love hath come to cheer and bless mankind,
To raise, uplift, and let oppressed go free,
To heal sick souls, restore sight to the blind,
To give to all the law of liberty,
For whoso drinks the universal cup,
Through him shall all mankind be lifted up.

Song.

Love came to me with a crown,
I took it and laid it down.

    Love came to me and said,
    " Wear it upon thy head."
" 'Tis too heavy, I cannot wear it,
I have not strength enough to bear it."

    Then my soul's belovèd spake,
    Saying, " Wear it for my sake."
When lo ! the crown of love grew light,
And I wore it in all men's sight.

I.

Who loves as I love, faces worse than death,
For he will find but endless misery
Unless for ever in his soul he saith,
O Lord, let my will with thy will agree.
There is no safety but in God's right hand,
For man's own will is his worst enemy,
Unless upon the rock of faith he stand,
He can by no means gain the victory.
What courage have I then who meet these woes,
And dare all things to set earth's children free !
What shall be said to one who overthrows
And buries Babylon beneath the sea ?
Shall not the tree of life to her be given ?
And her heart's home be builded high in heaven ?

II.

We meet no more, 'tis best we should not meet,
Yet all thy virtues live within my soul,
Thy holy will my life doth now control,
We have become a dual-heart complete
In all its attributes, each must repeat
The other's song; we are ensphered and whole,
We may not change; though seasons onward roll
Our pulses beat in time, our spirits greet.
Nay, would I lose that deathless memory?
O God, I thank thee that love cannot die,
That thy decrees do work eternally,
And souls are one on earth as in the sky,
Though silence fall between us; destiny
Works out the plan of God revealed on high.

Song.

Forget the singer, but take the song,
. Forget the giver, but take the gift,
May the love of God keep your souls from wrong,
And the comforting truth your hearts uplift.

My spirit watches o'er thee as it might
Watch over thee if I had long been dead;
Thou art revealèd to my inner sight,
Thy thoughts I know, and in thy footsteps tread.
This power I have is gained by sacrifice
Of outward life, and shows which others prize,
But what can weigh against thee? Or what price
Be overmuch that gains me thy dear eyes?
Nay, I must feel their light at any cost;
My life be guided by their sacred rays,
And what I lose for them were better lost,
Let all things die that cannot win their praise.
As my heart's virtues from thy soul proceed,
Let them return to bless thee at thy need.

His Soul Speaks.

WHAT can life give us, loved one, any more?
We have known all the joy that man can know,
And now methinks we must know all the woe—
Woe, woe, and dreary waiting on life's shore—
Our drooping wings, alas ! no longer soar,
We count the weary tides that ebb and flow,
We count the weary days, and as they go
Rejoice that fewer days are left in store.
Oh waiting death, that art the gate of life !
Oh life, that sometimes seems a living death !
Oh peaceful death !   Oh days of ceaseless strife ;
Oh what can reconcile ye ?   Oh vain breath !
E'en as a vapour ye shall pass away
Forgotten, for man's life is but a day.

Her Soul Answers.

NAY, love, though all things die, yet thou shalt live;
I swear it by my immortality
That I to thee immortal life will give,
And thou shalt in the heavens dwell with me.
Are not our heart-beats measured by the stars?
The very hairs are numbered on thy head.
Who rests in God, nor time nor change debars,
All things shall be as His own soul hath said:
Let him declare, and lo! the thing is done,
Thy faith alone is wanting, or thy sight,
Thou art but blind, the fight is fought and won,
And thou by choice still dwellest in the night,
And God alone doth know why this should be;
Alas! must I lose Paradise and thee?

Song.

WITH thee my life is calm, and pure, and blest;
Without thee, 'tis a sea filled with unrest.

She Declares Herself.

I AM the child of faith, and I shall be
A stumbling block to many.   Who sees me,
Sees how the human holdeth the divine—
Shall see Christ's body in the bread and wine,
And know the Triune, Father, Spirit, Son,
And how these Three are joined as Three in One ;
Shall see through all the universal plan
How spirit worketh for the inner man,
How souls though fallen in the deep abyss
May through pure love attain their heavenly bliss ;
Shall see how Wisdom, Mother of our Lord,
Revealeth unto man th' incarnate Word,
How blessed love, the pure, the undefiled,
For ever cometh in the form of child —
Born of a virgin love in purity,
It brings to all a new virginity.
Shall know why truth was ever crucified,
Until revealed as Bridegroom with the Bride

L

And how the earth must then from struggling cease,
Forgetting all its woes in endless peace,
And how all souls who would receive the Son
Must know the Bride, receiving two in one,
And how the Bride reveals the Mother's grace
Pervading nature, though none see her face.
This mystery made manifest in me,
(As in all flesh the highest truths shall be,)
As diamond hidden in the earth's dark mine,
When brought to light with heavenly truth doth shine.
Thus doth my soul its inner light put forth,
Thus shines the bright Aurora from the North:
For every soul is born with its own light,
And where the soul shines there is no more night,
But endless peace born of an endless day ;
And angels sing for joy when that new ray
Pierceth the dome of heaven ; then is born
A star among the ages—a new morn
Of gladness—for from earth is then redeemed
A chosen one, whose garment is not seamed,
Another soul triumphant wings its flight
Among the glories of eternal light.
There is no law for those who dwell within
The realm of causes, they cannot know sin,
For God doth work through them, and they do know
The sign by which pure spirits come and go.

Children of life who nevermore know death,
Their life is hidden, but their living breath
Is as a two-edged sword unto mankind,
Death unto death, life unto life.   They bind
All nature with their universal love ;
They are the chosen prophets of the Dove ;
They dwell for ever in the promised land,
Where milk and honey flows, a blessed band
Of spirits, and to them the earth is given,
They rule it by the laws revealed from heaven,
They are the blessed meek, and those who mourn
For all earth's sins too heavy to be borne,
They shall be comforted ; the Spirit saith,
" Come unto me, let him that hungereth,
Eat and be filled, for here is righteousness ;
Uplift the weary, and all sinners bless."
O holy garden ! O thrice Holy Lord !
Thy sabbaths I enjoy, filled with thy word,
Thy virtues in me evermore increase,
I more and more obey the voice of peace.
Grant, O my Father, that this joy of mine
May penetrate all hearts and through them shine ;
Grant that all eyes may holy vision see
Of God in man, of man's divinity :
That woman, mirror of the blessed sun,
Be lifted up, her reign has now begun

As Reconciler, Comforter, and Dove,
The all-embracing, universal love,
The help-meet, who has waited until man
Had worked his portion of the Father's plan;
Though still rejected, she, and she alone,
Is the Great Builder's polished corner stone.
'Tis the Lord's doing, marvellous in our eyes:
Echo His praises through the earth and skies.

Valediction.

WHAT has been, is, and shall be again;
I know not how, and I know not when,
But sometime in the ages thou wilt call
And I will answer; waking from thy thrall,
Thou wilt behold me, and with glad surprise
And wonderment rejoice with beaming eyes,
For I shall be the vision of thy dream,
Upon my forehead thy love's crown shall gleam,
Clothed with the radiant light as with the sun,
Bright rainbow hues all melting into one
White light, then flashing as with inward fire;
Within my hands Apollo's golden lyre.
My lips inspired, seraphic strains shall sing,
Whose rhythmic melodies shall echoing ring

Within thy soul, and thou, O King of men,
Shalt then behold thy kingdom, and again
Receive thy crown, bestowed by love's own hand;
Then shalt thou dwell within thy chosen land,
High Priest, and Ruler, King by right divine,
Melchizedek—beneath thy tree and vine
Where none can thee molest nor make afraid,
Talking with God and with the Holy Maid
Whose lips unknown delights to thee reveal,
And thou shalt then all mysteries unseal,
For thou art worthy, called by thy own name,
Henceforth belovèd, born of spirit flame.
Upon thy brow the shining diadem
Whose rays reveal thy glory, and in them
All souls may find the light if they will see,
And thou wilt show to them the mystery
By which we fought, and, conquering, overcame;
To all the door is open, and the same
Victorious laurel waits for every one
Who braves temptation; and when work is done
The labourer may rest, for God hath said,
" To him that overcometh, on his head
Shall be the crown of life; he rules with me
Upon my throne throughout eternity;
The morning star shall unto him be given,
And he shall enter the repose of heaven."

"The Lord gave, and the Lord hath taken away.   Blessed
be the name of the Lord."

JOB i. 21.

Chorus.

OUT of each heart there went a flame,
And rose till it came to the Great White Throne,
And there the two were made as one,
And as those flames ascend, aspire,
God accepteth the gift of fire,
And giveth instead His own bright Name.

Epilogue.

WITHIN THIS BOOK LIE EMBALMED

Two Mortal Hearts,

ABOVE IT HOVER

Two Immortal Spirits.

———•◦‡◖‡◦•———

*" Blessed are the dead which die in the Lord:
Yea, saith the Spirit, that they may rest from their
labours; and their works do follow them."*

Rev. xiv. 13.

AMEN.

CONTENTS.

THE THREAD RESUMED.

INTERLUDE.—*The Valley of the Shadow.*

PART III.

The Reality.

PART IV.
The Triumph.

INTERLUDE.—*The Tenor Voice.*

THE THREAD RESUMED.

INTERLUDE.—*Echoes.*

CONTENTS. 175

PART V.

Valediction.

London :
Chaloner & Cooke,
Printers.

www.ingramcontent.com/pod-product-compliance
Lightning Source LLC
Chambersburg PA
CBHW031114020726
47495CB00007B/2195